- BOOK 2 -
THE VOLTAGE VAMPIRES

M.K. RADICAN

 **Canaby Press**

Canaby Press, LLC | Sheridan, Wyoming

Cover design by Marcus Alexander Hart
using artwork by upklyak, brgfx, macrovector, and Freepik.
https://www.freepik.com/upklyak
https://www.freepik.com/brgfx
https://www.freepik.com/macrovector

Canaby Press, LLC
30 North Gould Street | Suite R
Sheridan, WY 82801
CanabyPress.com

This is a work of fiction. Names, characters, places, and events are either a product of the author's imagination or are used fictitiously. Locales and public names may sometimes used for atmospheric purposes. Any resemblance to actual persons, living or dead or undead, or to businesses, events, institutions, or locales is unintentional.

Zombie Reconstruction Squad: Book 2
The Voltage Vampires / M.K. Radican
Paperback Edition 3

Paperback ISBN: 979-8671477702
eBook ASIN: B088LPT8VP

Books By M.K. Radican

ZOMBIE RECONSTRUCTION SQUAD
- BOOK 1 -
THE GOOPY GHOSTS

ZOMBIE RECONSTRUCTION SQUAD
- BOOK 2 -
THE VOLTAGE VAMPIRES

ZOMBIE RECONSTRUCTION SQUAD
- BOOK 3 -
THE SMOKY SKELETONS

ZOMBIE RECONSTRUCTION SQUAD
- BOOK 4-
THE WATERMELON WEREWOLVES

TABLE OF CONTENTS

CHAPTER ONE

VIRTUAL THROW UP

Beyond the rusted, creaky gates of the Pootville Cemetery, in the shadow of a weeping willow tree, there was a crumbling old crypt. Inside the crypt was a spiral staircase that led down, down down, deep underground to a very creepy, but very special tomb. It was lit by weird, glowing blue mushrooms that grew out of the walls and floor, but that wasn't what made it special. It was special because of the huge marble arch that stood in its center.

Urg the kid zombie walked around the arch on his stiff legs. His skin was a mottled, greenish blue and his clothes were all ragged and stinky. He scratched his dusty black hair and blinked his big, bloodshot eyes.

"This is terrible!" he said. "I need to go home, but I still can't unlock the door to the Zombie Zone!"

Urg's friend Emilio studied the gateway. Emilio was ten years old, and super smart. He crossed his arms over his skinny chest as he looked through the empty arch at their pal Roach on the other side. Roach was an eight-year-old ball of energy with rosy cheeks and scabby knees. She had a strange device strapped to her face. It looked like a pair of safety goggles that someone had painted black, covering her eyes like a blindfold. The straps that wrapped around her head made her crazy red hair stick out in every direction. She bounced on her toes and grinned.

"One dozen water balloons, coming up!" she shouted.

She spun her arms in the air and jumped around like a wild monkey. Emilio ignored her. He was too interested in the arch to pay attention to her weirdness. It looked like nothing more than an empty doorway now, but if Urg could power it up, it would turn into a portal between the Human World and his home in the Zombie Zone.

"Don't worry, Urg," Emilio said. "We'll help you get that gateway open."

Way up on the top of the arch, a gravely voice laughed. Emilio looked up to see a gray stone gargoyle peering down at him with glowing orange eyes. The first time the statue had revealed it was alive, Emilio was shocked and amazed. Now he was just annoyed.

Carlyle the Gargoyle stretched his stony bat wings and shook his head. "You know perfectly well I won't let you open the portal to the Zombie Zone until Urg locates his misplaced body part. It's too dangerous to leave them here in the Human World!"

That was true. Zombie body parts were full of spooky magic that people could use to make creepy monsters. Somebody had already used Urg's lost nose to unleash boogery ghosts that slimed the whole town! If he left something else behind, who knows what kind of weird monster would appear next?

Urg crossed his arms. "Well it would be easier to find my missing part if you'd tell us what it is," he said. "We don't even know what we're looking for!"

"You're smart kids," Carlyle said. "I'm sure you'll figure it out."

He crouched down and his orange eyes blinked out as he turned back into a lifeless statue.

"Oh, we'll never find it!" Urg groaned. "I'm doomed!"

Emilio gave him a pat on the shoulder. "Don't worry, buddy. Let's just do an inventory of body parts to see what's missing." He put his hands on his ears. "Do you have two ears?"

Urg touched his ears. "Two ears, check!"

Emilio held up his hands. "Ten fingers?"

Urg looked at his dirty hands and slowly counted from one to ten. "Ten fingers, check!"

Emilio tapped his sneaker on the ground. "Ten toes?"

"Hmm," Urg said. "Let me look."

The zombie sat on the floor and pulled off his shoes. As soon as he did, a green cloud wafted off his feet that smelled like a skunk soaked in garlic oil. Emilio grabbed his nose and gagged.

"Put them back on!" he choked. "Before I barf!"

"But I have to count my toes!" Urg said.

"Count them fast!" Emilio shouted, holding his mouth.

Urg quickly counted ten toes and slipped his shoes back on. Emilio fanned the air and took a cautious breath. On the other side of the tomb, Roach continued hopping around and swinging her arms.

"And there's the pitch!" she said. "Oooh, right in the teeth! Take that, Bozo!"

Emilio walked over to her, careful to avoid her thrashing.

"Hey, Roach," he said. But Roach couldn't see or hear him. The device she had strapped to her head covered her eyes and pressed headphone speakers against her ears. Emilio tried again, but louder. "Hey, Roach!"

He tapped her shoulder and she jumped away from him with a terrified scream!

"Aaagh! It's too real! The evil clowns are touching me!" She shoved the mask up over her forehead. Her eyes were wide and crazed. She blinked a few times and smiled.

"Oh, hi Emilio. Hey, Urg. I forgot you guys were here."

Urg pointed at the device strapped to her head. "What is that thing?"

Roach took it off and showed him. "This? It's my virtual-reality gaming headset. I'm playing the greatest game ever! It's called *Throw Up!*"

"Is it a game about Urg's feet?" Emilio asked, rubbing his nose.

"No way," Roach said. "It's a game about throwing stuff!" She wound up her arm and made an imaginary pitch. "You start with normal things like baseballs and footballs, but then you get to throw weird stuff."

"Like what?" Emilio asked.

"On level five you throw giant meatballs and loaded plates of spaghetti!" Roach said. "Right now I'm on the last level. Evil clowns are invading, and I have to squash them by throwing whole elephants! It's intense!"

"Sounds fun!" Urg said.

"Oh no, it's not just fun," Roach said. "It's the *most fun thing ever!*" She pushed the game back down over her eyes and ears and cracked her knuckles. "Get over here, Jumbo. Those clowns are going down!"

She started leaping around and swinging her arms, but then she stopped and screamed. Emilio jumped back and gasped.

"What's wrong?" he asked. "What happened?"

"Oh no! The evil clowns got her!" Urg cried.

Roach ripped the game off her head, causing her hair to puff out in all directions. She growled at a blinking red light on the top of the device.

"Arg! The battery just died!" she moaned. "And right when I was about to beat the last level! This is the worst day of my life!"

"Mine too," said a stony voice. The kids all looked up at Carlyle staring down at them with his hands on his ears. "Can't you see I'm trying to sleep? Why don't you noisy brats go play somewhere else?"

Urg shook his head. "I'd go play at my house in the Zombie Zone if you'd let me open the portal," he said. "I have to go home! My parents must be worried sick about me!"

The gargoyle grinned. "Oh, I'm sure they are. That's why I've locked the gate to the Transit Tomb from their side, too. I wouldn't want them coming here to get you! That would be cheating!"

"Wow," Emilio said. "That is like, next-level mean, dude."

"I'm not mean. I'm just doing my job," Carlyle said. He pointed at Urg. "Little zombie, if you ever want to go home, I suggest you stop bothering me and go find your missing body part!"

CHAPTER TWO

THE GRAVEYARD DRONES

Urg, Emilio, and Roach emerged from the underground Transit Tomb and into the tall, dead grass of the creepy old cemetery. Emilio blinked and rubbed his eyes as he looked at the purple sunset.

"Oh my gosh," he said. "I didn't realize we had been down there so long. It's almost dark already."

Roach scowled and shook her VR headset. "This stinks! A whole day of progress on this game lost because of a dumb dead battery!"

"Wait, do you guys hear that?" Urg said. He put a hand to his ear and listened. Emilio and Roach listened too.

"I hear a weird buzzing sound," Emilio said.

"It sounds like bees," Roach agreed. "Or mosquitoes. Or beesquitoes!"

"What in the world is a beesquito?" Urg asked.

"It's a bug that sucks your blood and then turns it into honey." She wiggled her fingers and spoke in a scary voice. *"Bloooooood honey!"*

Urg took a frightened step back. "Is that a real thing?"

Emilio shook his head. "It is so not a real thing," he said. "Roach is just messing with you."

"Oh, that's a relief," Urg said. "I was scared for a—"

Something big and blue flew past Urg with a roaring buzz! He yelped and jumped back, but a red thing buzzed right behind him! He screamed and ducked as a green blur roared over his head.

"Beesquitoes are real!" Urg cried. "They want to turn me into blood honey!"

Emilio watched the flying objects as they whipped around a dead tree and headed off in another direction. "Those aren't beesquitoes," he said. "Look!"

Urg and Roach looked where Emilio was pointing to see three quadcopter drones chasing each other through the cemetery. One was blue, one red, and one green. They were shaped like sleek squares with a propeller on each corner. Roach hopped up on a crumbling tombstone to get a better view.

"Wow, look at those things go!" she said. "They're so fast!"

The drones buzzed around the tombstones in neat formations, rising and diving and whirling in spirals. The red one blasted through a stone arch in an old tomb, cutting through a blanket of spider webs with its spinning propellers. The green one followed it through, but the blue one just dropped out of the air and crashed in the tall weeds.

The two remaining quadcopters raced toward a fallen tree leaning against a crypt. The green one swooped under it and launched back into the sky. The red one tried to follow, but its four blades sputtered to a stop. It fell and rolled end over end as it crashed into the dirt.

The final drone sailed around a tall tombstone and zoomed in for a landing in front of three kids standing near the cemetery gates. There were two boys and a girl, each holding big remote controls. The girl jumped and cheered as she picked up the green drone.

"Yes! I win again!" she said. "I'm the best pilot in the whole family!"

The taller boy frowned. "No way! I want a rematch!"

"Yeah, me too!" the shorter boy said. "That was so unfair!"

He trotted off to fetch his crashed drone. Roach bounded over to the three kids, followed by Emilio and Urg.

"Don't listen to these complainers," she said to the girl. "You totally won. That was some sweet piloting!"

"Thanks!" the girl said. She smiled and gestured at the two boys. "I'm Greta Sikorsky. These are my brothers, Blake and Rex."

"Nice to meet you," Emilio said. "I'm Emilio, this is Roach, and that's Urg."

"Roach? Urg? Those are weird names," Blake said.

"Roach is short for Rochelle," Roach explained.

Blake nodded. "Oh, that's not so weird."

"And Urg is short for Urgablurgablurg," Urg noted.

Blake scratched his head. "That's actually even more weird."

"Why are you three flying your copters here?" Emilio asked, changing the subject. "The old cemetery is a strange location for a race."

Rex returned with the two crashed drones. "No way! This place is perfect!" He pointed to all of the cracked and mossy tombstones sticking crookedly out of the ground. "There are so many things to fly around. We made up our own obstacle course!"

Blake looked out over the graveyard. "Although our course might be a little too long. Our batteries keep dying before we can finish it."

"Yeah!" Rex agreed. "I totally would have won if my quadcopter hadn't run out of juice!"

Greta frowned. "I also started with a full charge and barely made it over the finish line. These drones are fun, but the battery life is terrible!"

"Oh man, I can relate!" Roach said. She shook her virtual reality game angrily. "Dead batteries ruined my game of *Throw Up!*"

Blake picked up his blue drone. "Well, it was cool meeting you, but we need to go and recharge."

"Yeah, me too," Roach agreed. She turned to Emilio and Urg. "Come on. Let's go to my house so I can plug in." She waved to the Sikorskys. "Later, dudes!"

They all said their goodbyes and squeezed out through the widely spaced iron bars of cemetery gate. The gate was locked, but very bad at its job of keeping people out.

Dusk turned the sky to darkness as Roach led Emilio and Urg down the quiet streets toward her house. On the way they passed through a park, and noticed some kids gathered in the middle of a grassy field, setting up some equipment.

"Hey, what are they doing?" Urg asked.

"I'm not sure," Emilio said. "Let's go find out."

As they approached, one of the kids in the field pointed up at the sky.

"Taurus the Bull should be over there," he said. He gestured a different direction. "And hopefully we'll be able to see Orion's Belt over there."

Roach squinted up past the clouds. "A bull and a belt in the sky?" she said. "You're crazy. All I see are stars."

The boy laughed. "The bull and the belt *are* stars. They're constellations."

"Of course," Emilio said. "Constellations are imaginary pictures you can make by connecting stars with lines, like a dot-to-dot puzzle."

"That's right," the boy said. He held out his fist for a bump. "I'm Samir, president of the Pootville Elementary Astronomy Club." He nodded at a girl to his side. "This is our vice-president, Jenny."

Emilio introduced his friends. Samir gave Urg a concerned look. "Are you okay? Why is your skin blue?"

"Don't tell him you're a zombie," Emilio whispered. "He'll freak out!"

"I, uh... I'm blue because I'm cold," Urg said.

"But it's summer vacation," Samir said. He waved his arms in the warm air. "The weather is beautiful."

"He grew up in a volcano," Roach said. "He has to wear a coat if the temperature dips below a thousand degrees."

Samir pinched his nose. "And why does he smell so bad?"

"It was a spoiled milk volcano," Urg said. "Extra chunky."

Samir seemed skeptical, but before he could ask any more questions he was interrupted by Jenny.

"Samir, stop goofing off and help me set up." She took a long telescope out of a protective case and attached it to a tripod. "We'll be lucky if we can see any stars at all tonight. There's so much light pollution!"

"Light pollution?" Urg asked. "I'm confused. How can light get polluted? You can't dump trash in light."

Samir adjusted the telescope as he explained. "I know it sounds weird, but light can actually *be* a type of pollution for us star gazers."

Jenny pointed to the yellow glow of lamp posts around the park. "It's easier to see stars when the sky is very dark. With all these bright lights on, we can barely see anything!"

"We keep asking the city to turn them off for us, but they won't listen," Samir said. "It's super annoying!" He closed one eye and peeked through the telescope. "But at least we can still spot the brightest—"

Samir cried out as a blinding white light blasted into the air.

"Argh!" Jenny shouted. "What's going on? Now it's even brighter!"

Roach squinted toward the beaming shafts cutting through the sky. On the other side of the park she saw a brightly lit theater with four searchlights on the sidewalk outside. Each light was gigantic! Huge circular lamps, almost as big as her mom's truck. The lights slowly pivoted back and forth, dragging columns of light across the starry sky like enormous flashlight beams.

Urg squinted and shaded his eyes. "Those lights are so bright! What are they for?"

"It looks like there's a concert starting at the theater," Roach said. "The lights must be to get people's attention."

"I wonder who's playing," Urg said.

Emilio looked past the sweeping searchlights. "The sign says 'Undead Metal Massacre.'"

"That sounds like a rock band!" Roach said. "And an awesome one, too!"

A smile crossed Urg's blue lips. "Oh my gosh. An undead rock band!" He jumped up and down in excitement. "They must be zombies! Maybe they can help me get home! Let's go find out!"

He ran off toward the theater, leaving Emilio and Roach with a very confused Samir.

"Did he say zombies would take him home?" Samir asked. "What does that even mean?"

"I dunno," Roach said. "Who understands milk volcano kids, right?" She grabbed Emilio by the arm. "Come on, let's go!"

With that, the two of them ran off, chasing after Urg.

CHAPTER THREE

ROCKED TO DEATH

Roach and Emilio ran across the park and found Urg outside the theater. He was so excited he was doing a weird little dance on the sidewalk.

"This is so great!" he said. "I'm going to meet an undead band! After the show they'll take me home to the Zombie Zone with them for sure!"

He spun around and around, laughing with joy until he noticed a poster near the door. He stopped dancing and his blue face drooped in a frown.

"Oh no! This is terrible!" he moaned. "The Undead Metal Massacre show has been canceled! Look!"

He pointed to the poster. Sure enough, a big red banner had been pasted right across its center that said "CANCELED!"

"That's weird," Roach said. "Why are they using the search lights to get everyone's attention if the show is canceled?"

Emilio took a closer look. The poster was a photograph of three fancy looking ladies in puffy white dresses with feathery wings. They didn't look like zombies at all.

"This isn't the Undead Metal Massacre," Emilio said. He peeled up the bottom of the CANCELED banner to reveal some words that had been covered up. "Hmm, it says this band is called the Acoustic Tooth Fairies. It looks like they were supposed to play here tonight."

"Oh! I guess the Undead Metal Massacre took their place," Urg said. He jumped up and down with excitement. "Oh boy! I can't wait to meet them! Come on!"

He rushed into the crowd of people flooding through the doors. The theater was huge, with plush red seats and a balcony up above, all facing a black curtain stretched across the front of a big stage. Urg, Emilio, and Roach found three seats right in the first row. Spotlight beams raced around the auditorium, gliding over the people and the walls and coloring them with bright purple, green, and orange light.

"We got here just in time," Emilio said. "The show is starting!"

The sound of a squealing guitar filled the theater. Everyone looked toward the huge stage as the black velvet curtains opened, revealing the Undead Metal Massacre!

On one side of the stage, the guitarist played heavy metal riffs on his electric guitar. On the other side, a keyboard player pounded out notes so fast his fingers were a blur! And right in the middle, the drummer hammered on an electronic drum set, making spooky sounding digital beats. Each one of them had gross green faces. They staggered around and groaned into their microphones, singing songs about brains.

Urg shouted over the loud music. "Wow, it really is a zombie rock band!"

Emilio squinted and shook his head. "I don't think so," he said. "Check out their arms."

Urg took a closer look at the band. Their faces were green and creepy looking, but their arms were the colors of normal human skin.

"Oh no!" Urg cried. "These guys aren't real zombies at all! They're just people in makeup pretending to be zombies!"

"That's lame," Roach said. "I don't want to listen to *pretend* zombies." She crossed her arms and frowned. "I'll bet they don't even have real worms in their hair!"

The spotlights swirled in crazy patterns as the Undead Metal Massacre continued to thunder through their jams. Emilio bounced in his seat.

"I know you guys are disappointed they're not real zombies," he said. "But you have to admit, this band rocks!"

Roach shrugged. "Yeah, I guess I could get into this." She jumped up on her chair and started wildly thrashing her head to the music, throwing her red hair in crazy spirals.

Urg smiled and did a stiff little dance.

"Honestly they're better than a real zombie band," he said. "A zombie guitarist's rotten fingers always fall off before they finish their solos."

Emilio wrinkled his nose. "That's... really gross, actually."

Just then, the wailing of the electric guitar cut off with a loud *pop* and a flash of light!

Roach stopped thrashing her head and fell back into her seat.

"Hey, what happened?" she asked. "Did the guitarist lose his fingers?"

"Eww! I hope not," Emilio said. "Maybe his instrument just came unplugged."

"No it didn't!" Urg cried. "Look!"

Emilio and Roach looked where Urg was pointing and gasped in surprise. A weird monster was attacking the guitar player's amp! It was shaped like a bat, with a furry body and webbed wings, but it was way too big to be a bat!

"What is that thing?" Roach shouted. "It looks like a goose in a bat costume!"

"Why would a goose wear a bat costume?" Urg asked.

"So it can go trick or treating for bread crumbs. Duh," Roach said.

A spotlight shined on the creature, giving Emilio a better look. Its body was skinny and bony, covered in dark blue fur. With a sizzly screech, it opened a jaw full of pointy metal teeth and bit the top of the amplifier!

"Whoa!" Urg said. "What is that thing doing?"

Emilio's eyes went wide. "I think it's eating!"

The monster screeched happily as it gnawed on the amp, sucking jiggling bolts of electricity out of the equipment and into its body.

"It *is* eating!" Emilio said. "And it's getting full!"

Just a few seconds ago the monster had been skinny and dark blue, but now it looked totally different. Its whole body glowed with a crackling yellow light, and its little belly bulged. It opened its mouth and let out a huge belch, spitting hot white sparks across the stage.

"It sucked all the electricity out of the amp!" Roach said. "It's like some kind of voltage vampire!"

"And it's not alone!" Urg shouted. "Look out!"

People in the crowd screamed as a dozen more voltage vampires flew into the theater!

One of the little monsters landed on the keyboard and sunk its fangs into the power cable. Three more of them attacked the electric drum set. Even more of them circled around the spotlights high above, swooping in to take big slurping bites of electricity! As the vampires began to glow with energy, all the lights buzzed and went dim.

"They're eating all the power in the building!" Emilio cried.

Pretty soon the whole theater was totally dark except for the glowing yellow shapes of the electric bats flapping through the air. The audience panicked and shouted, pushing each other in the darkness as they tried to run away. In the confusion people started to bump and shove Emilio, Roach, and Urg.

"Hey! Be careful!" Emilio squeaked.

"Ow! You stepped on my foot!" Urg cried.

"Watch it, lady!" Roach barked. "Get your butt out of my face!"

29

"Put on your gloves and catch the vampires!" someone screamed. "Don't let them get away!"

"Gloves?" Emilio shouted. "Who said that?"

He squinted into the darkness, but he couldn't see who had spoken. He couldn't see anything! Somebody bumped into him so hard he almost got knocked down!

"Urg! Roach!" he shouted. "Where are you?"

"Over here!" Roach said. "Oof! Stop pushing!"

Emilio tried to move toward her, but a panicked man plowed right into him! He almost lost his balance, but he tumbled against another body in the darkness. People kept bumping and jostling him, turning him around and around until he was dizzy.

"Roach! Urg!" he called out. "Help!"

He struggled to stop moving but he got caught up in the crowd of people and swept right out the door! His feet twisted under him and he fell and rolled to a stop on the sidewalk next to Urg and Roach. They both looked trampled and woozy.

"Whoa, what happened?" Urg said, holding his wobbly head.

"I don't know," Roach said. "But I want to go on that ride again!"

CHAPTER FOUR

THE ELECTRICITY EATERS

The last few people in the audience ran out of the theater and into the street. Everyone was in a panic, totally terrified of the tiny creatures that had attacked the concert. Roach jumped to her feet and pointed to the building.

"Oh my gosh!" she cried. "Look at that!"

Urg spun around and covered his face.

"What is it?" he asked. "More monsters?"

"No! Even better!" Roach said. "It's a power outlet!"

She ran to the outside wall of the theater, where there was a row of heavy-duty power outlets. Most had searchlights connected to them, but one outlet was open. Roach took her virtual reality device out of her backpack and plugged it in.

"Finally!" she said. "I can charge my headset and finish my game of *Throw Up!*"

Emilio shook his head. "Roach, how can you think of your game in the middle of a voltage vampire attack?"

Roach shrugged. "My teacher says I have a very short attention span."

Before Emilio could reply, somebody screamed, "Look out! The monsters are coming!"

Urg, Emilio, and Roach all turned to see ten glowing bats fly out of the theater! The creatures beat their wings and flew in big circles around the street. One of them perched on top of a streetlight and bit the bulb like an apple! Sparks crackled as the bat sucked all of the electricity, making the light go dark.

"It's happening again!" Emilio said. "The vampires are eating all the power! Look!"

He pointed to the four giant searchlights. The monsters landed on them and clamped on with their giant fangs. With a sizzle of electricity and a sparking *glug glug glug* they slurped down the power. The lamps went dark and the bats grew bigger and brighter.

"Oh no, they're everywhere!" Urg said.

He was right. The vampires were biting the traffic signals and the lights on the nearby stores. They drank the energy from the theater's blinking sign and even from the cars driving down the street. Within a few minutes, the whole town had gone completely dark! The monsters squealed and spit sparks as they took off and flew away into the night.

"It's a total blackout!" Urg cried. "This is terrible!"

"I know!" Roach agreed. "Now my game won't charge at all!"

"Roach, stop messing around!" Emilio said. "This is serious!"

"It sure is! I'll never get to play the final level if those monsters keep stealing all the power," Roach said. She stuffed her headset back in her backpack. "We have to stop them!"

"Stop them?" Urg said. "We don't even know what they are!"

Emilio pondered it. "I think I do. Carlyle the Gargoyle said Urg was missing a body part. The last time he lost a part, someone used it to create goopy ghosts."

"That's right!" Urg said. "Do you think somebody is using my lost part to make voltage vampires?"

"Obviously," Roach said. "We didn't have a single monster attack in this town before you showed up and started dropping body parts like a baby drops goldfish crackers."

Urg frowned. "Sorry about that."

Emilio walked around Urg, looking at him carefully. "Hmm. Which one of Urg's parts could someone use to make vampires?"

"Probably his wings," Roach said.

"But I don't have wings," Urg noted.

"Ah ha!" Roach said. "That proves you lost them!"

Emilio pinched his eyes. "Roach, Urg never had wings. You can't lose something you never had."

Roach nodded. "That's what my mom says when people say I've lost my mind."

Urg scratched his dusty hair. "Hmm. It's definitely not wings, but what parts do those monsters have that I have?"

Emilio thought about the creatures flying around the street and biting onto all the lights. "That's it! The vampires have teeth! Urg, did you lose a tooth?"

"Let's see!" Roach said. She grabbed Urg's lips, pulled his mouth open and took a look inside. "You're right! There's a tooth missing!" She winced. "But the zombie bad breath is still there! Blech!"

She let go and backed away, holding her nose. Urg sniffed his breath.

"It smells okay to me," he said. "I just brushed my teeth last month!"

"Gross. No wonder they're falling out," Roach said.

Emilio snapped his fingers. "Hey, I just remembered! When we were trying to figure out the mystery of the goopy ghosts, Roach accidentally punched you in the mouth and knocked out your teeth!"

Roach rolled her eyes. "Wow, you guys. I said I was sorry. Can we just let it go?"

"Oh my gosh, Emilio's right!" Urg said. "I thought I put them all back in, but I must have missed one!"

"And I'll bet somebody found it and used it to make voltage vampires," Emilio said.

"But who would do that?" Urg asked. "And why?"

"I don't know," Emilio said. "But it's up to us to figure it out!"

"Heck yeah!" Roach agreed. "The Zombie Reconstruction Squad is on the case!"

Emilio looked around the darkened street. The people from the concert had run away, leaving them all alone. He pointed toward the park.

"The vampires flew off that way," he said. "Maybe if we find them we can find some clues."

"And get my missing tooth back so I can go home!" Urg said. "Let's go!"

He ran off down the road with Emilio and Roach right behind him. Without electricity, everything in town had gone totally dark and silent. The only light came from the stars and the moon, and the only sounds were quiet "oooh"s and "ahhh"s drifting out of the darkness.

"Wait," Emilio said. "Do you guys hear that?"

Roach put her hand to her ear. "Yeah! It's coming from over there, in the middle of the park."

"Let's go check it out!" Urg said.

They walked toward the dim light of a camping lantern with its flame turned all the way down. Next to the lamp, a few moving shapes were gathered around a long tube pointing at the sky.

"Hello?" Emilio called out. "Who's there?"

A voice came back from the shadows. "It's us. Samir and Jenny."

As Emilio's eyes adjusted to the murky light he saw the Pootville Elementary Astronomy Club and their telescope.

"Hey, what are you guys doing hanging out in the dark?" Roach said. "It's a blackout. Go home you weirdos."

"Home? Now?" Samir said. "No way! This has turned into a perfect night for stargazing!"

Jenny looked into the telescope.

"Oooh!" she said. "What a gorgeous view of the Lyra constellation! I've never seen it so clearly."

"Can I see?" Emilio asked.

"Sure! Take a look," Jenny said. She stepped out of the way and Emilio peered into the eyepiece.

"Hmm, that's strange," Emilio said. "Should the stars be moving?"

Urg gasped. "Those aren't stars!" he said. "Look!"

Everyone looked up into the clear, dark night to see three glowing spots racing across the sky.

"It must be those vampires flying away!" Roach said.

"You're right!" Emilio agreed. "We should follow them! They may lead us to whoever has Urg's tooth!"

"Yeah!" Urg cheered. "Then we can get it back and I can go home!"

"And maybe we can fix the blackout!" Emilio added.

"And I can finally charge my game!" Roach said. "Let's quit yakking and go catch those little monsters!"

CHAPTER FIVE

THE EYES IN THE SKY

Roach, Emilio, and Urg left the park and chased after the tiny bright spots flying high in the air. The streets were eerily quiet and dark as they ran through the town.

"Hey, that's weird," Urg said. He pointed up at the sky. "The lights are getting bigger!"

Emilio shook his head. "They're not getting bigger, they're getting closer! And fast!"

"Look out!" Roach screamed.

They all ducked as three shapes zoomed by right over their heads! A blue one, a red one, and a green one.

"Oh man," Emilio said. "We weren't chasing voltage vampires at all. It was just those drones again."

The quadcopters flew in a circle, each one shining bright white headlights that cut through the darkness. They all came in for a neat landing at the end of a dark alley. The Sikorsky kids were all there with their remote controls. Blake leaned against a fence. Greta sat on a big black trunk. Rex was perched on a garbage can. Roach winced and waved her hand under her nose.

"Dude, you need to hit the showers," she said. "You smell like someone barfed in your shoes."

"It's not me!" Rex said. "It's this trash that stinks." He thumped on the side of the plastic can he was sitting on. "And besides, it doesn't smell as bad as your friend here."

Emilio frowned. "Wow. Rude! I just took a bath this morning."

"Not you," Rex said. "Him!"

He pointed to Urg. Flies buzzed around the zombie's head, drawn in by the stink of decay. Urg sniffed at his shirt and stuck out his tongue.

"Blah! He's right," Urg said. "I do smell worse than a garbage can."

Emilio shook his head and grumbled. "Well, it's still rude."

Greta hopped off the trunk she was sitting on and opened it up. The inside was lined with little compartments, each filled with different parts.

"Hey, what's all that stuff?" Roach asked.

"This? Oh, it's just the accessories for our drones," Greta said. "Check it out." She pointed to a few sections. "These are extra propellers, in case one gets broken or lost. And these are cameras we can attach. And here are the chargers."

Urg looked into the trunk. "What are those gloves for?"

Blake took a pair of heavy black rubber gloves out of the case. "Oh, those are mine. I dropped my charger and kinda broke it. It still works, but sometimes it gives me a shock! I wear the gloves for safety."

"It doesn't sound very safe to me," Emilio said. "You should get a new charger."

"And you should mind your own business," Blake said.

"Wow, you're rude too," Emilio said. "It must run in the family."

Urg searched the dark alley. There was nothing but empty brick walls and a few trash cans. He frowned. "Well, it doesn't look like those monsters are anywhere around here," he said. "We should keep looking."

"But we have no idea where they went," Emilio said.

Greta looked frightened. "I'm sorry, did you just say *monsters?*"

"Yeah!" Roach said. "Little creepy ones that suck your blood and turn it into honey!"

Emilio shook his head. "No! Those are beesquitoes. And beesquitoes aren't even real. You made them up!"

"Oh. Right. I forgot," Roach said. "The monsters we're looking for are voltage vampires! They eat electricity."

Greta seemed skeptical. "And those are real?"

"Yeah!" Urg said. "Crazy, right? We have to find them and stop them!"

Emilio looked in the trunk of equipment and saw three big tablet screens next to the cameras.

"Hey, I have an idea," he said. "Could you guys fly your drone cameras up high so we can see the whole city at once? Maybe then we'll be able to see where the voltage vampires went."

Greta picked up a camera and attached it to the bottom of her green drone. "Of course! Using the cameras is super fun. Right guys?"

"For sure!" Blake said. He attached cameras to the other two drones. "Rex and I just charged all of our batteries, so we should be able to go really high."

Rex turned on the tablets, showing the views from each camera. "I bet I can fly higher than you losers!"

"You're on!" Greta said.

She grabbed her remote control and her green drone took off. Blake and Rex activated theirs, and all three quadcopters roared up into the sky. Emilio, Urg, and Roach watched the tablets, searching the videos for any glowing monsters.

"This is cool!" Emilio said. He pointed at the screen with the live feed from Greta's drone. "I can see the Astronomy Club looking at stars in the park."

"Hey, check this out," Urg said. "Rex's copter is over by the Pootville Theater. It looks like the band is doing something."

The screen for Rex's drone showed the Undead Metal Massacre in the street outside the darkened building. They were next to their tour bus, setting up some kind of equipment.

"What is all that stuff?" Urg asked.

"I can't tell," Emilio said. "It's too dark. Rex, could you fly closer?"

Rex's controller let out a loud beep. "Oh no," he said. "Sorry guys. My battery is nearly dead."

"But Blake said you just charged them," Urg said.

"We did," Rex agreed. "But they run down even faster when we're using the cameras. Those things take a lot of juice!"

Greta's control beeped, then Blake's.

"Our batteries are almost gone too," Blake said. "If we don't land we'll crash!"

"Wait!" Roach shouted. She grabbed the screen for Blake's drone and held it up. "Look at this!"

Everyone looked at the screen to see a parking lot full of people. All around them, bright orange lights glowed and flickered.

"Those lights look like the voltage vampires!" Urg said.

"You're right!" Emilio agreed. "I know where that parking lot is. Let's go check it out!"

Emilio ran off down the street, followed by Roach and Urg.

"Wow, they didn't even say thank you," Greta said.

"I know, right?" Rex muttered. "And they said *we* were rude!"

CHAPTER SIX

THE ACOUSTIC TOOTH FAIRIES

Emilio, Roach and Urg ran toward the place where they saw the flickering orange lights on the drone's camera.

"It should be right over here," Emilio said. "Come on!"

The three friends darted around a big brick building and up a short driveway into a parking lot. There were no cars parked there, but a bunch of people were gathered in the shadowy darkness. The only light came from a series of bamboo tiki torches stuck in the ground surrounding the edges of the pavement.

Urg looked around, confused. "Where are the voltage vampires?" he said. "We saw them on the camera feed, but they're not here."

"They must have already left," Roach said.

"I don't think so," Emilio said. He pointed to the crooked rows of torches. "It looks like we made a mistake. Those flickering lights we thought were monsters were actually little flames."

"Oh butts," Roach cursed. "That doesn't help us at all."

Urg watched the crowd gathering in the warm light of the torches. "This is really weird," he said. "Why are all of these people hanging out in a parking lot?"

"Maybe they're pretending to be cars," Roach said.

"Why would people be out at night pretending to be cars?" Urg asked.

"Because if they did it during the day, they'd get stuck in traffic, duh," Roach explained.

Emilio shook his head. "They're not pretending to be cars. I think they're here for a show. Look."

He pointed to a small stage set up in the middle of the parking lot, lit up by a circle of torches. Three women in white, puffy dresses were on the platform waving to the crowd. Their hair was all swept up and covered in glitter, and they had long fingernails painted with white polish.

"Thank you for coming to our surprise pop-up show!" one of the fancy ladies said. "We're the Acoustic Tooth Fairies!"

"Here's our first song," another lady said. "It's called 'Brush Your Teeth So Your Breath Won't Stink!'"

Roach elbowed Urg. "Pay attention, buddy. You could probably pick up a few pointers from this song."

The crowd applauded as the three ladies started their concert. One of them played an accordion, one played a banjo, and the third played a set of bongos.

Urg, Roach, and Emilio moved closer to the stage to investigate. As they got closer, they could see that the women had feathery white wings attached to their backs, and their dresses were covered with odd little things that looked like badly shaped buttons.

"Hmm. I've seen these ladies somewhere before," Roach said. "But I don't remember where."

"I do!" Urg said. "They were on the poster outside the theater. The one that said CANCELED on it."

Emilio nodded his head. "You're right. I wonder why they're having a concert in a parking lot."

Roach snapped her fingers. "Maybe they're pretending to be a drive-in movie so all the people pretending to be cars have something to look at."

"That makes sense," Urg said.

"It doesn't, actually," Emilio mumbled. The band finished their song and the crowd clapped politely. "Come on, let's go talk to them."

"Pfft, you can't talk to a movie," Roach said. "Now who doesn't make any sense?"

Emilio made his way to the edge of the stage, followed by Urg and Roach. The banjo player tuned her strings while the others checked their lyric sheets. The lady with the bongos gave them a friendly smile.

"Hello! Welcome to our outdoor concert!" she said. "Isn't this nice?"

"I guess so," Emilio said. "But weren't you supposed to be playing in the theater tonight?"

The banjo player frowned and angrily picked at her strings. "We were!" she said. "Our show had been planned for weeks, but as soon as that heavy metal band rolled into town we got kicked to the curb!"

Urg thought about it. "Oh, you mean the Undead Metal Massacre?"

"Yes!" the accordion player said. "The owner of the theater is a big fan of theirs, so when they showed up he canceled our show so they could use the auditorium instead!"

Emilio frowned. "Wow, that's so unfair."

The bongo player scowled and tapped on her drums with her long white fingernails.

"I know!" she said. "But now we get the last laugh!" She gestured around the parking lot. All along its edges, the buildings and houses were completely dark. "An electric rock band can't play during a blackout, but an acoustic band can!"

The banjo player smiled. "Now *their* show is canceled and *ours* is still on!" She shook a fist. "Take that, you dumb fake zombies!"

"Hmm. Would you excuse us for a second," Emilio said. He pulled Roach and Urg into a huddle and whispered. "Did you guys hear that?"

"Yes," Roach said. "She yelled it right in our faces."

Emilio shook his head. "Well, yeah. But I mean, these ladies were mad at the metal band for taking the theater away from them. What if they were the ones who ruined the show?"

Urg gasped. "You think the Acoustic Tooth Fairies released the voltage vampires and caused the blackout?"

"Maybe," Emilio said. "And if they did, that means they have your tooth!"

"But how can we know for sure?" Roach asked.

Urg thought about it. "Let's ask them some questions and get some clues."

"Good idea," Emilio said. "But we have to be sneaky about it so they don't know we suspect them."

"Got it," Roach said. She stepped away from the huddle and pointed at the band.

"Hey! Did you creeps steal my friend's tooth?"

Emilio pinched his eyes and sighed. "Roach, do you even know what 'sneaky' means?"

The Acoustic Tooth Fairies looked upset at the accusation.

"We would never steal a tooth!" the bongo player said. "All of our teeth come from respectable tooth dealers! We bought them!"

Emilio blinked. "Wait, what? You buy teeth? Why do you buy teeth?"

The accordion player smiled and waved at her big frilly dress. "We're collectors! Check it out!"

All of the band members moved nearer to the tiki torches, letting the flickering orange light spill across their costumes. Urg's eyes went wide as he got a closer look at them. Before he thought they had a lot of strange buttons stitched to them, but now he realized what he was really looking at.

"They're teeth!" he shouted. "Your dresses are covered with teeth!"

The banjo player brushed her skirt proudly. "Yes, they are! Aren't they wonderful!"

"Yeah, if you're an insane dentist!" Roach said. "What kind of freak collects people's teeth?"

The accordion player gasped. "People teeth? Oh, heavens no. We don't have any people teeth! That would be weird."

Emilio rolled his eyes. "And you people definitely aren't weird."

The bongo player sat on the edge of the stage and fluffed up her skirt, holding it to the light. "Here, let me show you some of my collection." She tapped a nail on a large, pointy one. "This is a tooth from a great white shark!" Her finger traced a long, curved tooth. "And this one is from a beaver." She adjusted her dress to show a tooth as big as her hand. "And this is a fossilized tooth from a T-Rex!"

Roach gaped at the collection. "Dang, an actual dinosaur tooth? That's the coolest thing I've seen all day." She nodded approvingly. "You know, I didn't like dresses before I met you ladies. But now I'm on board."

Urg looked at all the strange and mismatched teeth stitched onto the fabric of the banjo player's dress. "I can't even guess what animals these teeth come from. They're all so unusual!"

The banjo player smiled proudly. "We love to collect exotic teeth. The weirder the better!"

That gave Emilio an idea for a sneaky question.

"So, you like weird teeth?" he said.

The bongo player nodded. "Oh yes, very much!"

"You know what's the weirdest tooth of all?" Emilio said. "A zombie tooth!"

Urg scratched his head. "That's not so weird. I have whole head full of them."

He opened his jaw to show off his teeth, but Roach clapped a hand over his mouth.

"No you don't," she said. "Because you're a perfectly normal kid. Right?"

Urg blinked. "Oh! Right. I forgot. I'm not a zombie. I'm just a normal blue kid from an expired milk volcano."

The accordion player squinted at Urg's mottled skin in the dim firelight.

"How is any of that normal?" she asked.

"It's a long story," Emilio said. He stepped in front of Urg to hide him from the band. "But we were talking about zombie teeth. Do you happen to have one stitched onto your dresses anywhere?"

The banjo player just shook her head.

"Oh, no," she said. "A zombie tooth would be far too valuable to sew onto our costumes.

What if it fell off and we lost it! That would be a real bummer!"

Urg nodded sadly. "I can confirm. Losing a zombie tooth is a bummer."

The bongo player smoothed down her dress. "We keep our really rare and strange teeth in our special collection up in our apartment."

She pointed to a tall building across the parking lot and up to a window on the very top floor. Roach rubbed her hands together eagerly.

"Ah ha! Now we're getting somewhere!" She took a step toward the building. "We want to see this 'special collection' of yours. Let's go!"

The banjo player shook her head. "Um, no. I don't know if you kids noticed, but we're kind of in the middle of a concert here."

Someone in the crowd shouted angrily. "Is it really a concert? I'm beginning to think it's a fashion show!"

"Or a visit to a super boring dentist!" someone else added.

The audience started to boo and chant.

"We want music!" they yelled. "We want music! We want music!"

The Acoustic Tooth Fairies picked up their instruments and looked at each other with worried expressions.

"Oh gosh, they seem angry!" the bongo player said. "We should play a real crowd pleaser!"

The accordion player tapped a long nail on her front teeth as she thought about it. "I know just the thing!" She moved to the center of the stage and shouted out over the audience. "Our next song is called 'Flossing Is Awesome'!"

She counted off a "One, two, three!" and the band launched into song.

"Flossing is awesome!" the accordion player sang.

"Yeah yeah!" the others agreed.

"But not when it's a dance move," the accordion player continued. "Only when it's using a string to clean your teeth!"

Roach shook her head and covered her ears. "Now I understand why the theater owner canceled their show."

CHAPTER SEVEN

METAL IN THE STREETS

Emilio, Roach, and Urg went back to the park to think of a new plan to find the voltage vampires. They could still faintly hear the sound of the Acoustic Tooth Fairies singing their weird dental tunes in the parking lot nearby. Emilio paced on the grass. Urg sat on a bench. Roach hung upside down from a tree branch, shaking her VR game.

"What are you doing?" Urg asked.

"I had this great idea," Roach said. "If I turn my game upside down and shake it, maybe some extra power from the bottom of the battery will come out."

"That doesn't sound like a great idea at all," Urg said.

Emilio agreed. "The only way Roach is going to get her headset charged is if we figure out the mystery of the voltage vampires and end this blackout." He pointed to the tall building at the edge of the park. "If my guess is right, those three fairy ladies have Urg's rare zombie tooth up in their apartment. We have to convince them to show us their collection."

"Why don't we just go up there and take a look ourselves?" Urg said. "The Acoustic Tooth Fairies are still playing their concert. We could sneak in and investigate."

Emilio shook his head. "Um, no. Breaking into someone's house is super illegal, buddy."

"Really?" Urg said. "Weird. Zombies do it all the time. Usually it takes a lot of us pushing to break down the door, though. Come to think of it, when we do that the people inside always try to smash our heads open and kill us."

Emilio blinked. "Yeah, whenever possible we like to minimize getting killed."

Roach flipped out of the tree and landed on the ground with an awkward thump.

"Listen, there's no point in breaking in and getting our heads smashed open before we even know if Urg's tooth is there," she said. "First we should look in the window to see if we can spot it in their collection."

"That's a great plan!" Urg said.

Emilio shook his head. "It's a slightly better plan, but I wouldn't call it 'great.' Peeping in people's windows is really rude. What if we saw someone in their underpants?"

Roach stuffed her game in her backpack and rolled her eyes.

"Dude, do you want to be polite or do you want to find Urg's tooth?" she asked.

Emilio scratched the back of his neck. "Both, actually."

Urg squinted into the darkness at the Acoustic Tooth Fairies' window way up on the top floor of the apartment building.

"It's too far away," he said. "I can't see my tooth *or* anyone in their underpants. Even if I stand on my tippy toes!"

Roach gave him a pat on the shoulder.

"Don't worry," she said. "I have a plan! Come on!"

She turned around and ran off. Emilio frowned.

"Oh no," he said. "I don't like it when Roach has plans."

He chased after her. Urg followed, bouncing along on his stiff zombie legs. They caught up to Roach in the middle of the park with Samir and Jenny and the rest of the Astronomy Club. The club members were taking turns looking through their big telescope at the clear, dark night sky.

"This blackout is amazing!" Jenny said. She squinted into the eyepiece. "With all the city lights turned off, I can see stars I've never seen before!"

Roach stuck out her tongue. "Pfft. Stars. Whatever." She pointed at the top of the apartment building. "If you want to see something really cool, you should point your telescope in that window over there!"

Samir crossed his arms and shook his head. "No way. Looking in people's windows is rude," he said. "What if we saw someone in their underwear?"

"That's what I said!" Emilio agreed.

Roach shook her head. "Why are you people all so obsessed with underwear?"

Jenny finished looking through the telescope and moved to let someone else have a chance. Urg shuffled up and cut in line in front of the next person.

"Hey!" the club member said. "It's my turn!"

"I'm sorry," Urg said. "This will only take a second!"

He grabbed onto the eyepiece and turned the telescope on its tripod to point it toward the window. Samir gasped and screeched!

"Oh my gosh! Stop!" he cried."Don't touch it like that!"

Urg raised his hands and backed away, surprised by Samir's shouting.

"What's the matter?" Urg asked. He pointed to Jenny. "You didn't get mad when she moved it!"

Samir bent down and opened the long carrying case on the ground. He took out a pair of white cotton gloves and a soft white cloth.

"That's because Jenny knows how to handle a telescope!" Samir snapped. "You clearly don't!"

Jenny nodded in angry agreement. "You put your whole palm over the eyepiece! Now it's all smudged and dirty!"

69

Samir bent down and took a closer look at the lens.

"Eww! Gross!" he shouted. He carefully pinched something long and wriggly off the telescope. "You got a worm on it! Why was there a worm on your hand?"

Urg looked at his palm and shrugged. "That's weird. Usually all the worms stay on the inside."

Jenny gaped at him with horror. "Are you saying you have worms inside your body?"

"No!" Emilio shouted. He knew the Astronomy Club would freak if they found out Urg was a real zombie. "I mean, what he's saying is... um... the worms stay inside his hoodie."

"Why does he have worms in his hoodie?" Samir asked.

Roach laughed. "Because they'd get squished if he put them in his shoes."

Jenny stuck out her tongue. "You people are all really gross, you know that?"

Roach nodded. "Yeah, we get that a lot."

Samir pulled on the white gloves and used the cloth to carefully wipe all the zombie funk off the lens. He finished and smiled at his work. "There. Good as new." He nodded to the club member Urg had cut in front of earlier. "Okay, Caleb. It's your turn."

"Finally!" Caleb said. He squinted into the newly cleaned eyepiece. "I can't wait to get a look at this clear, dark sky!"

Just then a mechanical roar rumbled across the park and four bright white shafts of light blasted into the air! They swept back and forth, completely blotting out the stars. Caleb threw his hands up.

"Ugh! What now?" he cried. "I'm never going to get to see any stars!"

Emilio looked toward the source of the lights. They were coming from the ground near the theater on the other side of the park.

"I recognize those beams," Emilio said. "It's the searchlights from the Undead Metal Massacre concert!"

Samir took off his gloves and angrily threw them into the telescope case.

"Argh!" he shouted. "How did those dumb lamps get turned on in the middle of a blackout?"

Urg gasped. "If there's lights, that means there's power! You know what that means!"

Roach jumped up and let out a whoop of joy. "Yes! I can charge my game!"

Urg shook his head. "No! If there's power, the voltage vampires will come to suck it up!"

Emilio clapped a hand on Urg's back. "You're right! And when they do, they might lead us to whoever stole your tooth!"

Jenny looked at them, confused. "Wait, vampires and stolen teeth? What are you gross weirdos talking about?"

"No time to explain!" Roach said. "I have a game of *Throw Up* to charge!"

CHAPTER EIGHT

CAN'T STOP THE ROCK

Roach ran off toward the blazing searchlights to find a place to charge her VR game. Emilio and Urg chased after her. When they got to the theater, they found a group of heavy metal fans gathered near a big green bus with spooky purple lettering that said UNDEAD METAL MASSACRE. The mechanical roar they heard from the park was even louder here. Roach put her hands over her ears and shouted.

"What's that terrible noise?" she asked.

Emilio followed the sound and noticed a machine set up on the sidewalk next to the bus. A whole bunch of cables and wires were plugged into it, snaking away around the corner of the theater.

"It looks like an electrical generator," Emilio said.

"You're right!" a voice replied. "You're a smart kid!"

Emilio, Roach, and Urg turned to see a man wearing big sunglasses and a bright pink shirt. His face was smeared with clumpy green makeup.

"Hey, I recognize you," Roach said. "You're the keyboard player from the zombie band!"

The man nodded and wiggled his fingers in the air. "I sure am! They call me Jimmy Z, master of the keys! Are you kids here to see the performance?"

Urg shook his head. "I'm confused. I thought your show got ruined when the blackout happened."

Jimmy Z waved his hand and laughed. "No way! Those little power-sucking monsters can't stop our concert!" He pointed to the noisy machine next to the bus. "We always carry our own gasoline-powered electrical generator for emergencies like this. Now we're all ready to rock! Come on, the show is about to start!"

Urg, Emilio, and Roach followed Jimmy Z as he hustled off around the corner. Behind the theater, the band had set up a huge stage in the street, surrounded by speakers and bright, colored lights. The drummer's electric drum kit glowed and flashed as he pounded out a booming rhythm.

"Hello, Pootville!" the green-faced guitarist shouted into his microphone. "Are you ready to rock out, zombie style?"

The crowd cheered, and he turned up his guitar and started cranking out heavy metal riffs. Jimmy Z hopped up on stage and played loud, spooky pipe-organ melodies on his keyboard. Roach jumped up and down and thrashed her head to the beat.

"Oh yeah!" she shouted. "These guys rock my face off!"

The guitarist leaped around and wailed on his guitar, blasting out a wave of heavy metal noise. The music was so powerful Emilio could feel it vibrating in his chest. He covered his ears.

"It's too loud!" he shouted.

Roach shook her head. "Emilio, why are you such a grandma?" She turned to Urg. "You don't think it's too loud, do you?"

Urg opened his mouth to answer just as Jimmy Z played a deafening blast of organ noise. It was so loud that Urg's zombie ears blasted right off the sides of his head! He blinked and shrugged.

"It doesn't sound too loud to me," he said. "For some reason I suddenly can't hear anything at all!"

Emilio's nose wrinkled as he looked at Urg's greenish-blue ears lying on the sidewalk.

"I think I have a pretty good idea why," he said.

Roach crouched down and grabbed Urg's ears. "Eew! They're so squishy!" She dangled them under her own ears and turned her head from side to side like she was modeling jewelry. "What do you think of my new earrings? They're ears! They're ear earrings!"

Emilio stuck out his tongue. "Ugh. Sometimes I can't even believe how gross you are."

"What's the matter?" Roach said innocently. "You don't like ear earrings? How about ear earmuffs?"

She put Urg's ears in the palms of her hands and slapped them over her own ears. Emilio turned pale.

"I think I'm gonna throw up," he said.

"What was that?" Roach shouted. "Sorry, I can't hear you! I'm wearing ear earmuffs!"

Emilio closed his eyes. "Would you just give Urg his ears back, please?"

Roach huffed. "Ugh. Fine. You're no fun."

She took Urg's ears off her own ears and clapped them back onto the sides of the zombie's head.

"Ah! That's much better!" Urg said. He blinked and tipped his head, listening. "Hey, what's that buzzing sound?"

Emilio listened hard. The fake zombie band was still rocking out at maximum volume, but under the noise he could hear a faint buzzing.

"I hear it too," he said. He looked around for the source and noticed a bright light overhead. "Look!"

Roach and Urg looked up to see the quadcopter drones zooming over the audience. Each one had its camera pointed at the stage. Urg spotted three kids at the edge of the crowd near the theater wall.

"Hey, look," he said. "It's the Sikorskys. They must be recording a video of the concert."

"That's so cool!" Roach said. "Let's go check it out."

Urg and Emilio followed Roach as she bounded away from the stage and over to the RC pilots. Blake sat on their accessory trunk and Greta leaned against the brick wall of the theater. Both of them were watching the live video feed from their drones on their tablet screens. Rex was still perched on top of a plastic garbage can. He looked up at his copter as he flew it in big, swooping figure eights over the crowd.

"That's some pretty fancy flying!" Urg said.

"Thanks!" Rex said proudly.

Emilio watched the drone nervously as it sailed over the audience.

"Aren't you worried about hitting those people?" he asked. "If your battery dies your copter will crash into their heads!"

"Wow," Greta said. "You are such a grandma."

"Right?" Roach agreed.

Blake waved his hand. "Don't worry, we won't crash," he said. "Our drones are all fully charged. It's perfectly safe, Grandma."

Emilio threw his hands in the air. "Stop calling me Grandma!"

Urg looked around and sniffed. "Hey, do you guys smell something stinky?"

"Yes," Blake said. "It's you."

Roach snorted a lungful of air. "No, Urg is right," she said. "There's something even more stinky than him."

Emilio stepped closer to Rex. "Eww, nasty. The smell is coming from this garbage can you're sitting on! It smells like someone puked in it!"

Urg took a whiff of the can and stuck out his tongue. "Blah! You're right!"

Roach crossed her arms and shook her head at Rex. "Dude, every time we see you you've got your butt parked on a stanky trash can. Haven't you ever heard of chairs?"

Before Rex could answer, Greta grabbed her tablet with a gasp.

"Oh my gosh," she cried. "Look at this!"

She turned her screen around so everyone could see the view from her drone's camera. It was a close-up of the guitar player, shredding on his guitar on stage. He was so into his music he didn't even notice the creature creeping up behind him.

It was a big blue bat, doing a weird kind of crawl on its legs and wings. It opened its jaws and shrieked, revealing a mouth full of pointy metal teeth! Another one swooped down and perched on the keyboard. Two more dipped out of the sky and landed with heavy *thunks* on top of the tour bus.

"Watch out!" Roach shouted. "The voltage vampires are back!"

The dark, shadowy monsters screeched and flew over the audience. Everyone in the crowd started screaming and running away in terror!

"I don't get it," Urg said. "These bats are dark and blue. Why aren't they glowing like the others were?"

"Because they're not charged up yet," Emilio said. "Look!"

He pointed to the monsters as they flapped their long wings and landed on the band's electrical generator. They all screeched with happiness as they opened their huge, toothy jaws and bit onto the cables! There was a giant *zap* of electricity as bright yellow bolts of lightning arced out of the wires and into their mouths!

On stage, the Undead Metal Massacre's electric instruments sizzled and went silent.

"Oh no, not again!" Jimmy Z shouted. "Those monsters ate all of our power!"

The vampires snorted and gulped at the electricity coming out of the generator until the stage turned completely dark. All four of the big searchlights in front of the theater shut off, plunging the whole street into blackness. With all the lights off, the only things that could be seen were the bright yellow, sparking bodies of the fully fed voltage vampires. They spread their glowing wings and took off, streaking around in the sky like gigantic fireflies.

"They're getting away!" Urg shouted.

"Not this time!" Roach said. "Let's go catch us some electric monsters!"

CHAPTER NINE

VOLTAGE VAMPIRES ATTACK

Bright white sparks blasted off the vampires' beating wings as they flew through the darkened streets. Roach, Emilio, and Urg ran after them on the ground.

"Don't let them get away!" Emilio shouted.

The creatures were fast, but the Zombie Reconstruction Squad was faster. They chased the glowing yellow bats all through downtown Pootville.

"Where are they going?" Urg asked.

Emilio pointed to a big green building up ahead. "It looks like the monsters are headed toward the school!"

"Making us go to school during summer vacation?" Roach said. "Those things really *are* monsters!"

All four vampires screeched and squealed as they flew in a loop around the school playground. They swooped under the swings and circled the slide, racing and chasing after each other. One of the bats turned and flew straight toward Urg!

"I got ya!" Urg shouted.

The zombie jumped in the air and grabbed the attacking bat with both hands. As soon as he touched it, there was a loud *zap* and a blinding flash of white lightning! The vampire exploded, blowing both of Urg's arms clean off at the shoulders!

"Yow!" Urg cried. "That was a shocking experience!"

Emilio looked at Urg's arms flopping on the ground like two fish with elbows.

"Oh my gosh!" he said. "Urg, are you okay?"

Urg nodded. "I'm fine. When my zombie arms come off they can stick right back on."

"But our human arm's can't!" Roach said. "Emilio, watch out!"

The three remaining vampires flew high in the air and then dove toward Roach and Emilio!

"Don't let them touch you!" Urg shouted. He hopped up and down, looking helpless and silly without arms. "They'll blow you up!"

Emilio and Roach ran off in different directions, and the vampires split up to chase them. A smaller one went after Emilio. He tucked and rolled across the grass as the bat swooped right over him! In the blink of an eye, he was back on his feet running the other way, but the flying monster was too fast. It turned in a tight spiral around a tree and dove out of the sky at him!

"Emilio, look out!" Urg yelled.

But it was too late. The vampire pounded face-first into Emilio's back like a big winged dodgeball. A bright white spark flashed in the darkness as the bat exploded with a jolt of electricity! Emilio yelped as he was thrown to the ground.

"Oh no!" Urg cried. He ran over to his fallen friend. "Emilio! are you all right? Speak to me!"

Emilio sat up, looking dazed. There was a huge black burn across the back of his shirt. Wisps of gray smoke poured out of his hair, which was all standing straight up on end.

"Oof, I'm okay," he moaned. "But I feel like I got fang fried!"

On the other side of the playground, the last two vampires screeched and swooped as they chased after Roach.

"Come and get me, you blinking buttheads!" she taunted.

The first bat flapped its wings and shot toward her, but she ducked behind the slide. With a squealing cry, the vampire slammed into the metal rungs of the ladder! Roach shielded her eyes from the bright light as the bat exploded into a jolt of raging yellow electricity that raced up and down the slide before going dark. Roach puffed out her chest and pounded a fist into her palm.

"Yeah! That's what you get when you come after Roach Riggs!" she shouted. "Who else wants some of this?"

The last vampire squealed and dove out of the air at her, teeth first! It was the biggest one yet, almost as tall as her! Roach tumbled out of its way and ran across the moonlit playground. Anger sparked in the bat's eyes as it made a wide turn and rocketed straight toward her.

"Roach, watch out!" Emilio shouted. "It's right behind you!"

The scruffy little redhead darted toward the swing set with the vampire closing in fast. It was hot on her heels as she threw out her arms and dove through the dangling O-shape of a tire swing. Her skinny body crashed face-first to the ground on the other side. The monster chased her, but it was too big! When it tried to fly through the tire, its head fit, but its long wings folded back and got wedged in the hole, pinning them down to its sides. The tire swung as the vampire struggled and squealed, but it was stuck tight!

Roach's friends rushed to her side and Emilio helped her up. All three of them could see by the bright, sparking yellow light coming off the trapped creature.

"Roach, are you all right?" Urg asked.

"Heck yeah I'm all right," Roach said. She stepped closer to the snarling vampire's gnashing jaws and stuck out a thumb. "It's this clown you've got to worry about. He messed with the wrong eight year old!"

She raised a foot and gave the swing a powerful kick, sending it into a wild spin! The vampire screeched and struggled as the tire spun around and around.

Urg looked curiously at the dizzy monster. "I don't understand," he said. "Why did the other three vampires explode into electricity when they touched things but this one didn't?"

Emilio scratched his chin and looked at the swing. "Wait, I know!" he said. "It's because the tire is an insulator!"

Urg was confused. "The tire is a large reptile from Florida?"

"No no," Roach said. "You're thinking of an alligator. An insulator is the staircase at the mall that moves by itself."

Emilio pinched his eyes. "No! That's an escalator! An insulator is a material that doesn't conduct electricity." He pointed to the swing. "That tire is made of rubber. Rubber is a good electrical insulator, so it trapped the vampire instead of making it spark and release all of its power!"

Roach looked at Emilio blankly, then nodded.

"Um, sure. I knew that," she said. She turned to the captured monster. "You're not so tough now that you're all wrapped up in an escalator!"

"Insulator!" Emilio snapped.

"Whatever," Roach said. She reared back and kicked the tire again, sending it into another crazy spin.

Urg's face wrinkled with worry. "Um, Roach," he said. "That vampire isn't looking so good.

By the time the swing came to rest, the bat's tongue was sticking out and its eyes were rolling around in their sockets.

"I think you'd better stop spinning that monster around," Emilio agreed.

"Or what?" Roach said. She leaned in close to the bat's face. "It's trapped. It can't zap me. It can't do anything to me!"

The queasy bat hiccupped and barfed all over Roach! But the barf wasn't barf at all. It was a spew of blue electricity that crackled over her body, knocking her to the ground! The vampire faded away and totally disappeared as all its power poured out of its mouth.

Roach squealed and sat up, wiping glowing sparks off her clothes and out of her hair.

"Bleagh!" she snorted. "That thing hurled its lunch all over me!" She wrinkled her nose and gagged. "Aaugh! Now I stink like vampire barf!"

"It's time for *Throw Up!*" a voice said.

"I think I've had quite enough throw up, thank you very much!" Roach said. She blinked in confusion. "Wait, who said that?"

Urg nodded at Roach's back. "Your butt just said it's going to throw up!"

"Weird!" Roach said. "Usually all my butt says is, *faaaaaaaart!*"

Emilio put his face in his palms. "Wow. Okay. It wasn't your butt talking. It was the game in your backpack."

"Game?" Roach said. Her face brightened with excitement. "Oh yeah! My game!"

She whipped her VR headset out of her bag and strapped it onto her eyes.

"All right!" she cheered. "That vampire's electric puke charged up my viewer! I'm back in it, baby! I can finally beat this last level!"

Roach jumped around, swinging her arms and totally ignoring the boys. As Emilio watched her play, he was struck with an idea.

"Wait! This is a clue!" he said. "I think I know who has Urg's tooth!"

"You do?" Urg asked. "Tell me who it is!"

"I'll do better than that. I'll show you!" Emilio said. "Come on!"

He turned to run off, but Urg shouted, "Wait!"

Emilio stopped. "What's wrong? I thought you would be excited to find out."

"I am!" Urg said. "But before we go, um... could somebody please put my arms back on?"

CHAPTER TEN

THE SHOCKING REVEAL

In the darkened street behind the theater, a group of stragglers was still gathered around the Undead Metal Massacre's outdoor stage. Blake, Rex, and Greta Sikorsky's drones buzzed overhead, shining their lights over the small audience. The band was trying to play their instruments, but without power, their electric guitar, drums, and keyboard only made pathetic little noises.

"Ugh! When is this blackout going to end?" the drummer moaned. "This is the worst concert ever!"

"I'll say it is!" a voice in the crowd yelled. "You guys are terrible!"

The metal band squinted into the darkness to see who had shouted the insult. In the pale moonlight, they noticed a group of kids with a long telescope case.

"Hey, kid! Did you call us terrible?" the guitarist said angrily.

Samir and Jenny looked at the other members of the Pootville Elementary Astronomy Club and shook their heads in confusion.

"Us?" Jenny said. "We didn't say anything. We're just trying to go home." She gestured at the huge outdoor stage setup. "You kind of blocked up the whole street."

"Over here!" the voice yelled again. "We said you were terrible!"

The Undead Metal Massacre spotted three ladies wearing white, puffy dresses covered in teeth. Jimmy Z the keyboard player wrinkled his nose.

"At least we don't look like we rolled around on the floor after a boxing match!" he shouted.

Just then Emilio ran up to the stage, followed by Urg and Roach.

"Hey Jimmy!" he said. "I have an important announcement to make! Can I get up on stage with you guys?"

Jimmy Z frowned. "Sure. Take the whole thing," he said bitterly. "We don't need it. Without power, our show is totally ruined!"

"Serves you right!" the Tooth Fairy banjo player yelled. She pointed a fancy white fingernail at him. "You talentless fake zombies stole our theater! We were supposed to play here tonight before you showed up!"

Emilio jumped up on stage. "Everybody please settle down!" he shouted. "I know who created those voltage vampires and caused the blackout!"

Urg scratched his dusty hair and looked at the three ladies scowling angrily at the metal band. His eyes widened and he snapped his fingers.

"Wait! I know, too!" he said. "It was the Acoustic Tooth Fairies!"

The crowd gasped in surprise. All three of the Tooth Fairies shook their heads in denial.

"What? It wasn't us!" the bongo player said. "Why would you accuse us of such a thing!"

Urg rolled his eyes. "It's so obvious! You were mad because the metal band took the theater away from you. So you used the zombie tooth you stole for your exotic tooth collection to create voltage vampires to ruin their show!"

The Acoustic Tooth Fairies all huffed and crossed their arms.

"That's not true!" the bongo player cried. "Yes, we were upset about losing the theater, but we didn't cause the blackout!"

97

The banjo player patted the weird teeth on her dress. "And we don't even have a zombie tooth! Not on our dresses or in our collection!"

Up on stage, Emilio nodded. "I believe you," he said. Everyone turned to him for an explanation. "When the monsters first appeared at the concert, I heard someone shouting in the chaos. They said they were going to catch the voltage vampires, but first they had to put on gloves."

Roach studied the women's hands and their long, fancy fingernails. "Well if the person who caused the blackout was wearing gloves, these three are in the clear," she said. "They couldn't even fit their hands into oven mitts with those nasty lady-claws."

"Thank you!" the bongo player said. She looked at her nails and frowned. "I think." She shook her head. "No, actually, that was mean. I don't thank you at all."

Roach turned away from the Tooth Fairies and raked back her scruffy hair. "But you know who did have gloves tonight?" She lurched forward and pointed an accusing finger. "Samir from the Astronomy Club!"

Samir gasped and stumbled away from the shouty little maniac. He raised his palms and his eyes went wide. "What? Me? I didn't do anything!"

"Oh yeah?" Roach said. "Then why were you carrying those white cotton gloves?"

"Because I need them for cleaning the telescope!" Samir shouted. "They make sure I don't get fingerprints on the lenses when I polish them. I mean, seriously. Why would I want to create monsters? It doesn't make sense."

"Don't play innocent with me!" Roach barked. She pointed at Jenny. "You either! You're in this together!" Roach walked in a circle around them, staring them down. "You two were complaining about how the lights of the city were too bright just before those creatures showed up!"

Urg's mouth dropped open. "Hey, that's right! After the vampires sucked up all the electricity, the town went totally dark. You caused the blackout so you could see the stars more clearly!"

Jenny balled her little hands into fists. "We did not!" she cried. "Just because we benefited from the power failure it doesn't mean we caused it!"

"I believe you, too," Emilio said.

Roach shook her head. "You believe everybody. You're like, the worst detective."

"I believe them because they're telling the truth," Emilio said. He hopped down off the stage. "Whoever made the voltage vampires was using gloves to capture them." He gestured to Samir and Jenny. "The Astronomy Club definitely had a motive to black out the town. But if they released the monsters to eat all the power, why would they want to catch them?"

Roach crossed her arms. "Why would anyone want to catch them? All they do is explode and shock people and stink like barf."

"Exactly!" Emilio said. He took a sniff of Roach and winced. Her clothes still stank of electric puke. "When that vampire threw up on you the smell was terrible! And what else have we smelled tonight that's really stinky?"

Samir gasped and pointed at Urg. "It's your friend!"

"What?" Urg yelped.

"That's right!" the Fairy bongo player agreed. "That boy reeks! He caused the blackout!"

Emilio cleared his throat. "Uh, no. Wait."

"The blue kid did it for sure!" Jimmy Z cried. "He smells like five gallons of barf in a bag made of farts!"

"Stop it!" Emilio shouted. "I wasn't talking about Urg! I was talking about that!"

He pointed to the three Sikorsky kids, hanging around at the edge of the crowd with their remote controls. Greta and Blake were standing, but Rex was still sitting on that same garbage can. Roach sniffed her shirt and gagged.

"You're right!" she said. "The stink of the vampire puke on me is the same stink coming out of drone boy's trash throne!"

Rex shifted uncomfortably on top of the can. "You guys are crazy," he said. "So what if this garbage can smells? All garbage cans smell! They're full of trash all day!"

Greta nodded in agreement. "Yeah, don't go accusing us of anything. We have no reason to cause a power failure! We didn't want to ruin a concert or look at stars. All we wanted to do was fly our drones! You don't need a blackout for that."

Urg stuffed his hands in his hoodie pockets and shrugged. "That's true. I guess it wasn't them either."

Emilio walked over to the Sikorsky kids and raised a finger. "It's true that you have no reason to cause a power failure. But I think we've been looking at this mystery all wrong," he said. "I think the real question isn't 'Why did someone make vampires to suck up all the power?' but 'Where did all the power go?'"

Roach snapped her fingers. "Of course! That makes total sense," she said. She blinked. "Wait, no, that doesn't make any sense. I have no idea what you're talking about."

The Sikorsky kids squirmed as Emilio walked around them in a slow circle. "Think about it," he said. "Roach, you've been trying to charge your *Throw Up* game all night but haven't been able to find a single working power outlet." He pointed up at the quadcopters, still buzzing high in the air over the street. "But somehow these three have been able to keep recharging their drones."

Roach's mouth dropped open. "Oh my gosh, I get it now!" she said. She pulled her VR headset out of her backpack. "When that vampire electro-puked on me it charged up my game!" She pointed to the Sikorskys. "These kids must have had vampires hurling on their drones all night!"

Greta shook her head. "Okay, you sound like a crazy person. Even if we were going to capture electric bat monsters to make them throw up on our stuff..." She paused. "Which is something only a crazy person would say, I should note. How would we do it? Those things looked pretty dangerous."

"She's right," Urg said. "It would be impossible to catch them. The second you touch them they blow up and shock you! The only thing that can touch them is an alligator."

"Alligator?" Greta asked.

"He means escalator," Roach said.

"Insulator!" Emilio shouted. "He means insulator! The only way to catch a voltage vampire without discharging it is to use an object that doesn't conduct electricity."

Roach's eyes widened. "Wait! I just remembered something!" She darted over to the drone carrying case on the ground near Greta's feet. "Ah ha! Right here!" Roach reached into the compartments and pulled out something floppy and black. "Blake Sikorsky has a pair of heavy rubber gloves!"

Urg pointed at Blake's hands. "And his fingernails aren't too long to wear them!"

Blake looked around guiltily. "That's, uh... I don't know what you're talking about! I didn't do anything! I mean, even if I could catch a voltage vampire, where would I put it?"

Urg snapped his fingers. "Inside an alligator!"

"Yes!" Emilio said. He shook his head. "Wait, no! Ugh! Insulator! And you know what else is a good insulator besides rubber?" He thumped his knuckle on the side of Rex's garbage can. "Plastic!"

Rex wrapped his hands around the lid of the trash can. "What? No! This is just full of garbage! Stinky garbage nobody wants to look at!"

"I'll be the judge of that!" Roach said. "Move it or lose it, turkey!"

Before Rex could answer, Roach swung the long rubber gloves and smacked him in the face! With a surprised squeal he tumbled backwards off the garbage can, taking the lid with him. As soon as the bin was open, stink erupted from it like lava from a volcano!

Emilio grabbed his nose. "Aagh! Barf-o-rama!"

Urg gasped as he peered into the trash can. "Oh my gosh, look!"

The can was stuffed with five voltage vampires, all packed in and smooshed together. They screeched and wriggled their squashed wings as they tried to squeeze their way out. Roach looked at them with wide eyes.

"I can't believe it!" she said. "You guys have been making voltage vampires and catching them to use as barf batteries for your drones!"

Greta gaped into the can of struggling creatures with a shocked expression on her face.

"Oh my gosh," She said. "I had no idea! The boys have been charging our equipment all night." Greta turned to her brothers with total confusion. "Is all of this true?"

Rex stood up and brushed himself off with a resigned nod. "Yes. I'm afraid it is."

"But how?" Greta asked.

"We made the monsters with this," Blake said. He reached into his pocket and pulled out a nine-volt battery and a yellow molar. "Every time I touch the battery to the zombie tooth it makes a spark and a voltage vampire appears! After they suck up enough power to charge themselves, I put on my rubber gloves and catch them. Then I store them in this plastic trash can."

"My tooth!" Urg cried. "Give it back!"

He grabbed the rotten tooth out of Rex's hand, opened his mouth, and stuffed it into the hole in his gums.

"Aaugh! Gross!" Rex said. "Did you see what this kid just did?" He blinked at Urg's blue face. "Wait... are you..." He gasped. "Holy cow, it's a real zombie!"

Greta thrust a finger in her brother's face. "Don't change the subject, you dirty sneak!" she shouted. "Have you been making monsters barf on our stuff all night? That's nasty!"

"I know!" Rex said. "I'm sorry! We just wanted to have some fun flying our drones. We didn't mean to cause any trouble. And we certainly didn't mean to black out the whole town! It was an accident!"

Blake turned to the gathered crowd. "We're so sorry! Can you ever forgive us?"

Jenny shrugged. "Yeah, I totes forgive you," she said.

"For sure," Samir agreed. "Your blackout gave our club the best night of stargazing ever!"

The Acoustic Tooth Fairies smiled and fluffed up their dresses. "We forgive you, too. The power failure didn't stop us from having a good time tonight. Our torchlight concert was a big hit!"

Up on stage, Jimmy Z stood up and shook his fist. "Well we don't forgive you!" Everyone in the street looked up to see the fake zombie metal band pouting. "You ruined our show!"

"Twice!" the drummer added.

The guitarist gave his strings a pathetic twang. "Without power we can't rock out at all!"

Emilio took Rex's rubber gloves from Roach and pulled them onto his hands. "I think I have a way to fix that," he said with a smile.

He grabbed the garbage can with both hands, tipped it over, and kicked it as hard as he could! The can rolled all the way down the street and crashed into a fireplug at the far end. When the can hit the hydrant, its plastic sides split, spilling voltage vampires all over the sidewalk! The monsters staggered around with their tongues out, dizzy and wobbly from all the rolling. One of them groaned and put a wing over its mouth, then bent over and threw up! A sparking spew of blue electricity poured out onto some of the cables snaking from the metal band's generator. As soon as it did, the vampire disappeared and a bank of lights lit up across the top of the stage.

"It's working!" Urg said. "The vampires are barfing the power back into the wires!"

"Blech!" Roach said, holding her nose. "Monster puke stink!"

The other nauseated bats flew in the air in crazy, dizzy patterns, puking their guts out! One of them hurled onto a streetlight, and with a flickering spark, all of the lights came back on. Another one landed on an overhead power line and spewed all over it! The vampire disappeared as the Undead Metal Massacre's instruments came to life with a warm electronic hum. The guitarist raked his strings, sending a deafening blast of noise echoing through the street.

"All right!" he cheered. "The power's on, and so are we! Who's ready to rock!"

Roach shrugged. "I guess the third time's the charm!"

The band launched into a thunderous heavy metal riff. The crowd went wild as the last of the voltage vampires flew around overhead, disappearing as they ralphed up all their stolen electricity. The Astronomy Club clapped their hands to the beat. Even the Acoustic Tooth Fairies got into the music, dancing and shaking their costume wings.

Emilio smiled as he watched everyone having a good time. "Nice work, Squad!" he said. "We solved the mystery of the missing tooth and fixed the blackout!"

"Yeah we did!" Roach said. She wrinkled her nose. "I mean, the whole town smells like vampire puke now, but hey, nobody's perfect right?"

Urg grinned and tapped a blue finger on his yellow tooth. "And most importantly of all, I got my lost part back!" he said. "Now I can finally go home to the Zombie Zone!"

"Well what are we waiting for?" Emilio said. "Let's get to the Transit Tomb!"

CHAPTER ELEVEN

A DENTAL DISAPPOINTMENT

Deep under Pootville Cemetery, Urg, Emilio, and Roach entered the vault of the Transit Tomb. Urg rushed up to the huge stone arch, jumping up and down with excitement.

"Woo hoo! I found my missing part and I can finally go home!" he cheered.

"Yeah!" Roach shouted. "Get out of here, stinky!"

"Roach!" Emilio snapped. "Don't be a jerk!"

He turned to see Roach hopping around behind him with her VR headset strapped on her face. She tipped it up over her forehead and blinked.

"What did you say?" she asked. "Sorry. I was talking to my game. Now that I finally got my headset charged, I made it to the bonus level of *Throw Up* where you get to throw skunks!"

Emilio shook his head. "Never mind. Have fun."

Roach pulled her device back over her face and wiggled her fingers. "Get over here, you little black-and-white fart kittens!"

She ran off across the tomb, grabbing for skunks that weren't there. Emilio rolled his eyes and turned back to Urg.

"Well, Urg, it's been fun," he said. "Have a good trip home."

Urg nodded and smiled. "I'll miss you guys, but I'm so happy I'll finally get to see my family again." His smile drooped into a frown. "They must be so worried about me! I'd better get moving."

"Yeah, get out of here!" Roach shouted. "Before I throw you out!"

She pinwheeled her arms, flinging invisible skunks as she bounced across the back of the tomb.

"Is she talking to me or her game?" Urg asked.

"Who knows?" Emilio said. "I've stopped trying to make sense of her."

Urg grabbed a fistful of his dusty black hair. He gave it a sharp tug, and with a dry *pop*, the top of his head came right off, revealing his pink brain! Emilio looked away and covered his mouth.

"Dude, gross," he gagged. "You've got to warn people before you go pulling your brains out!"

"Sorry!" Urg said. "But I have to use my brain-print to unlock the door, remember?"

He stepped up to the arch and slapped his squishy brain into the bowl-shaped indentation in its side. A spark of purple lightning zapped across the empty gateway, then another. As the third bolt crackled through the opening, Emilio could see a faint image of the Zombie Zone on the other side. It was a neighborhood that looked a lot like his own, except the houses weren't neat and colorful like his house. They were all made of white marble and gray granite, like giant crypts. Each of the yards was dry and brown and overgrown, and there were long black hearses parked in some of the driveways.

"It's working!" Urg shouted. "The gate is opening!"

He tried to walk through the arch, but as soon as he reached it the purple crackles snuffed out and the graveyard neighborhood on the other side disappeared.

"Hey! What happened!" Urg cried. "Who closed the portal?"

A gravely voice answered. "I did, of course!"

Urg and Emilio looked up to see Carlyle the stone gargoyle lounging across the top of the arch. His eyes glowed orange as he peered down on them with a sneering grin.

"I'm not about to let you just walk out of here," the gargoyle said.

"Why not?" Emilio shouted. "You said Urg could go home when he found his lost body part, and he did!"

"Yeah!" Urg said. "Look!" He opened his mouth wide, revealing a full jaw of rotten yellow zombie teeth. "I found my lost tooth! They're all here now!"

Carlyle rolled his eyes. "Yes, and congratulations on that. But while you were out trying to find one missing body part, I'm afraid you lost three more."

"Three more?" Emilio cried. "Are you kidding me?"

Urg looked himself over, taking inventory. "I'm not missing anything, look!" He patted his body as he counted off. "Two elbows, two knees. One nose! Ten fingernails!" He grabbed his brain and slapped it back into his skull. "One brain! Everything is here!"

Carlyle chuckled with a noise like banging two rocks together. "Oh no. The things you lost are far more subtle than those parts of your gross anatomy."

"Hey, who are you calling gross?" Urg shouted.

"No no," Carlyle said. "'Gross anatomy' refers to the parts of your body large enough to see with the unaided eye. I didn't mean that your anatomy is gross." He considered it. "But now that you mention it, Your anatomy *is* gross. It works on a lot of different levels."

Emilio sighed with frustration. "Cut it out, Carlyle! Why do you always have to be such a bully?"

The gargoyle gasped, pretending to be offended. "Bully?" he said. "Me? I'm nothing of the sort! I'm merely a diligent gatekeeper. No zombie can return to the Zombie Zone without all of their body parts. I'm simply following the rules." He pointed at Urg. "This silly boy is the one to blame! All he had to do was pick up one little tooth and come back, but he managed to mess the whole thing up! He's the most careless, irresponsible, clumsy kid zombie I've ever—"

Carlyle's insults were interrupted by a rock bouncing off his stone forehead. He staggered back and yelped, rubbing a fresh chip just above his heavy eyebrows.

"Ouch!" he wailed. "Who did that?"

Everyone turned to see that Roach had taken off her VR headset. She shrugged.

"*Throw Up* is fun," she said, "but sometimes it's more satisfying to throw things in the real world."

The gargoyle shook his fist angrily. "Just for that I'm not going to tell you what parts Urg is still missing!" He settled down on his perch and huffed. "And without my help I promise, you'll never find them!"

"Challenge accepted!" Roach shouted.

Carlyle snuffed. "Well then, you'd better do it quickly. Because if someone finds the things Urg lost, they'll be able to make the scariest monsters yet!"

Emilio's eyes went wide. "Scarier than goopy booger ghosts?"

"Far scarier," Carlyle said.

"Scarier than voltage vampire bats?" Urg gulped.

Carlyle laughed. "So much scarier. I promise, when you see these new monsters you're going to pee yourselves!"

"Challenge accepted!" Roach shouted.

Urg blinked. "Wait," he said. "Do you mean you accept the challenge to pee yourself?"

Roach shook her head. "I don't even know. I kinda got lost in the moment there."

Emilio took a bold step toward the arch and pointed at the gargoyle. "We don't need your help anyway! We'll find Urg's missing parts on our own!"

Urg looked surprised. "You're still going to help me? Even after all the trouble I've caused?"

"Of course! You're our friend!" Emilio said. "We'll get you home if it takes our whole summer vacation. Right, Roach?"

"For sure! We've got your back, buddy!" Roach threw an arm around Urg's shoulders and one around Emilio's. "They don't call us the Zombie Reconstruction Squad for nothing!"

WHAT HAPPENS NEXT?

Find out in Zombie Reconstruction Squad
Book 3: The Smoky Skeletons!
Get it at CanabyPress.com!

ABOUT THE AUTHOR

When M.K. Radican isn't writing books about zombies, he's been known to write TV shows for Disney Channel and Disney XD. He lives in the Pacific Northwest and has a pet sasquatch named Larry MacHairy. One of these things is not true.

(The sasquatch is named Gary MacHairy.)

Made in the USA
Monee, IL
09 December 2020

51895542R00075